BEATRICE ALEMAGNA

THINGS THAT GO AWAY

Abrams Books for Young Readers
New York

In life,
many things go away.
They transform,

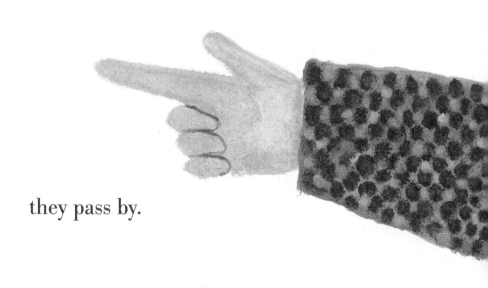

they pass by.

Sleep always departs.

A small wound (almost) always vanishes

without leaving a trace.

Music flies away.

Soap bubbles, too.

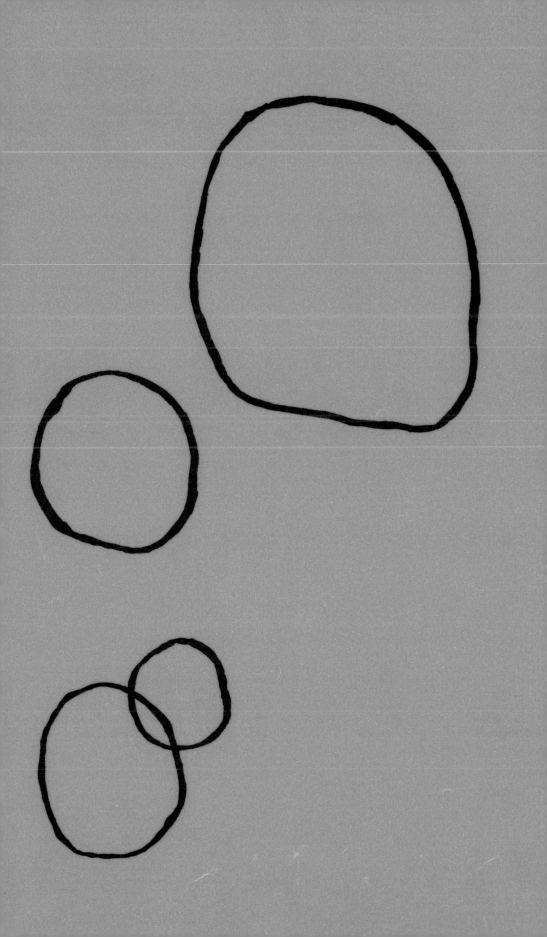

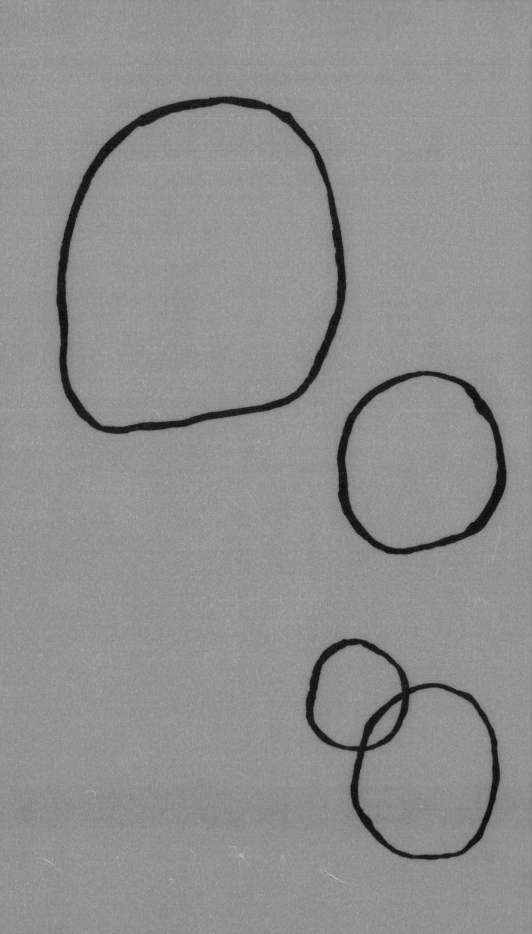

One day, lice (luckily)

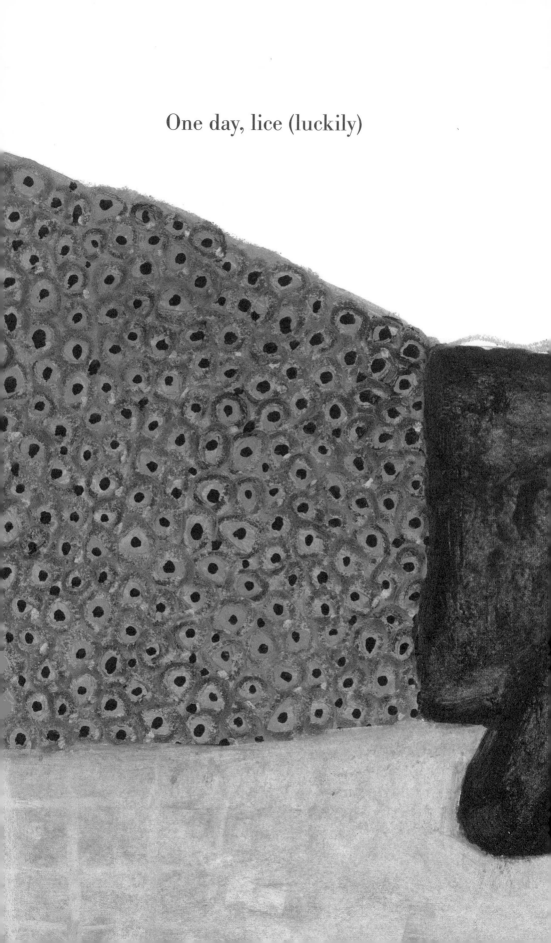

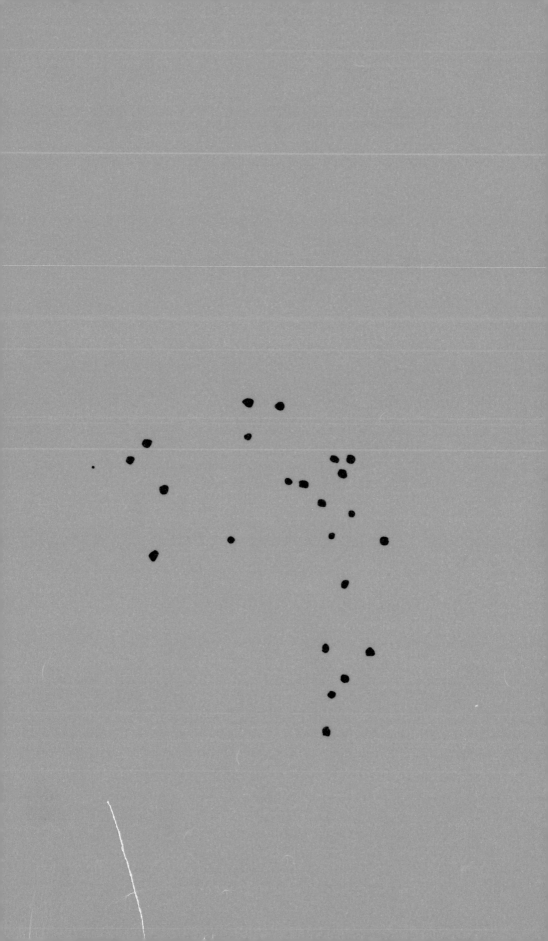

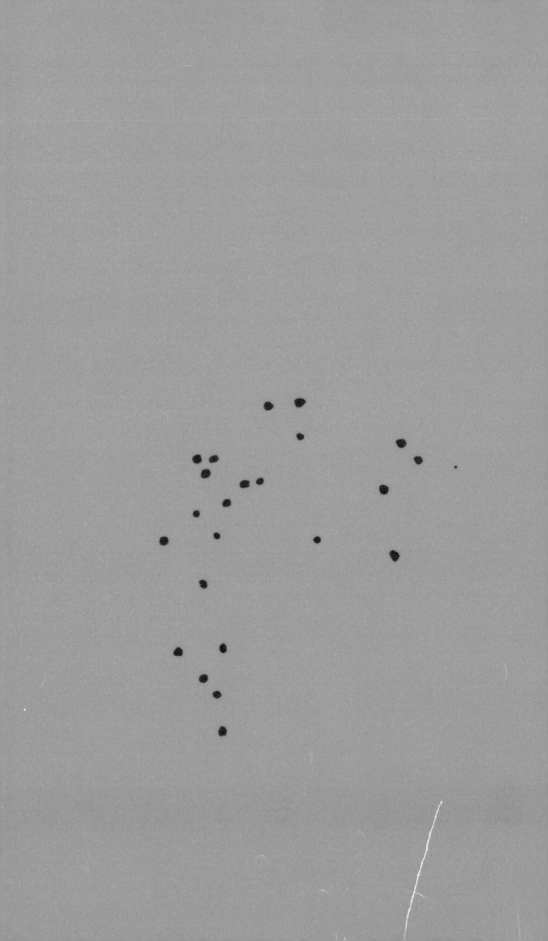

will also leave.

Dark thoughts fade,

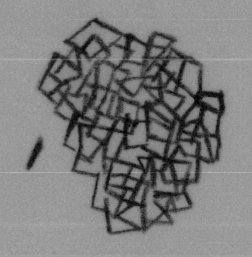

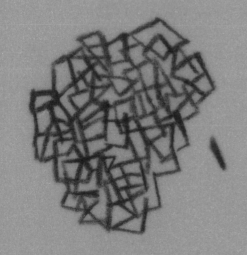

just like tears dry,

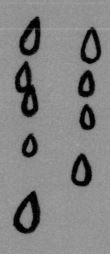

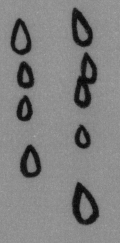

and the steam from a cup evaporates.

Bad weather goes away,

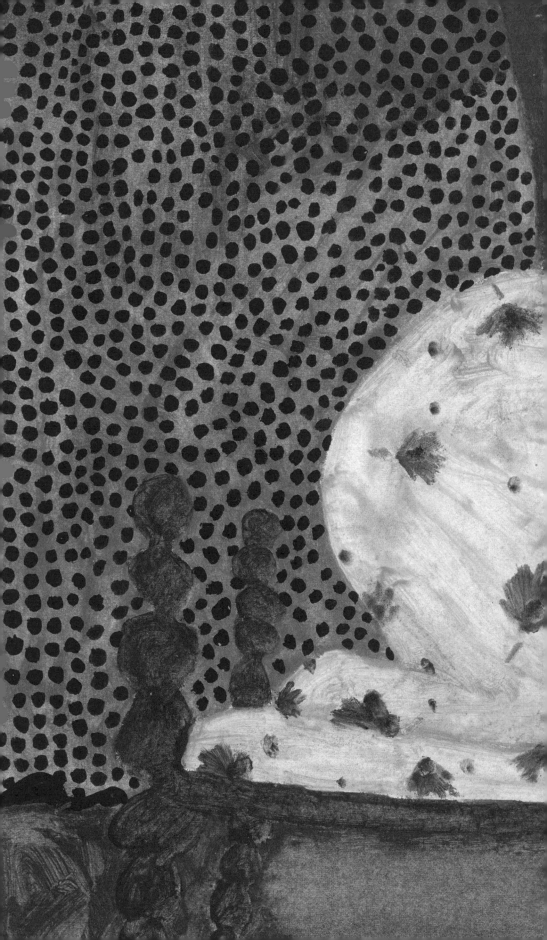

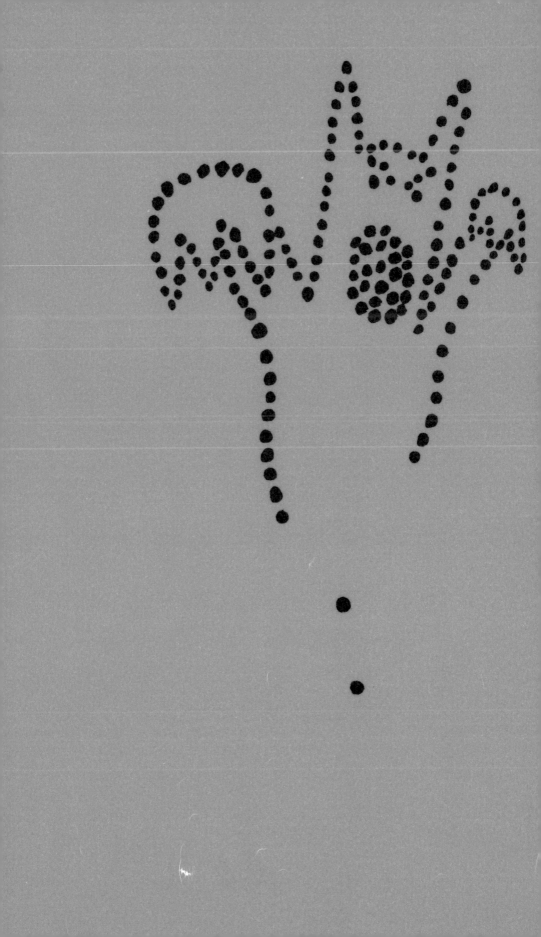

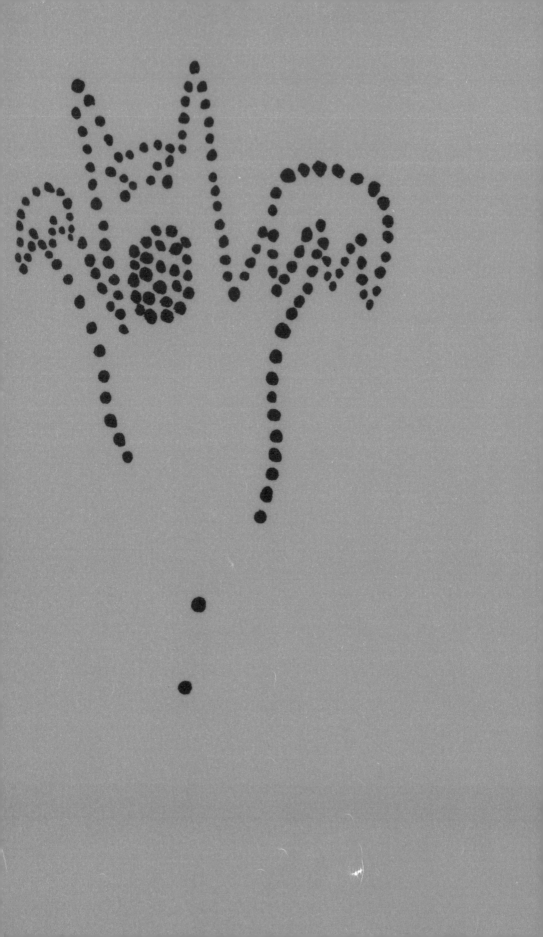

and so does fear.

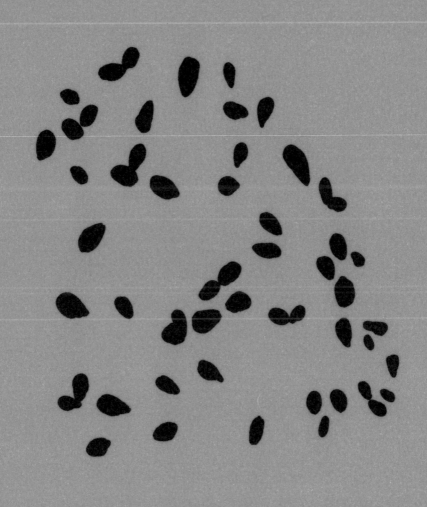

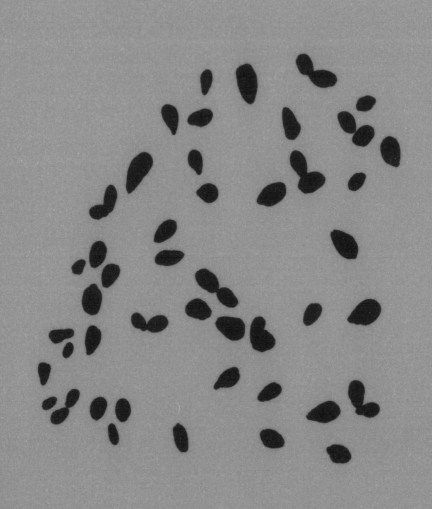

Leaves fall,

as well as hair, sometimes,

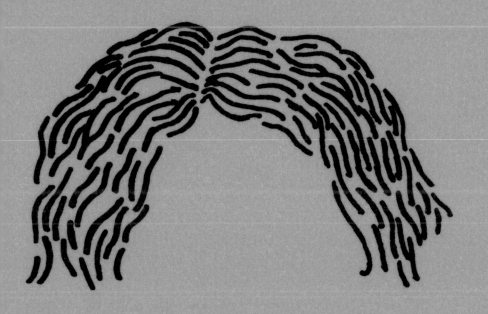

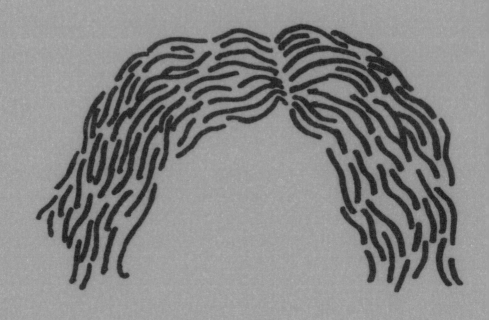

and baby teeth.

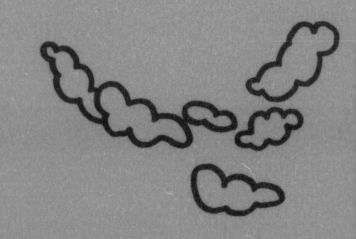

Dust disappears—but it
always comes back.

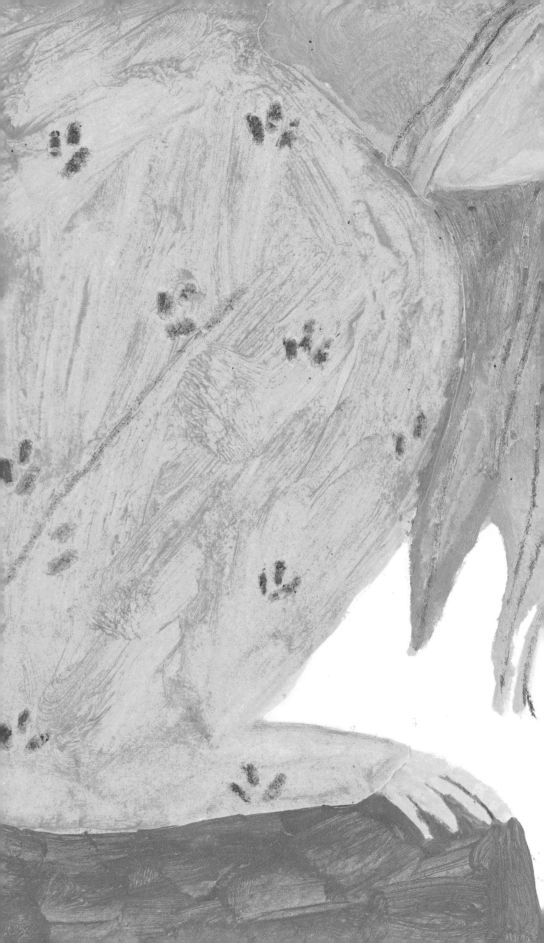

Eventually, everything passes,
moves on, or changes.

But one thing never goes away,

and never will.

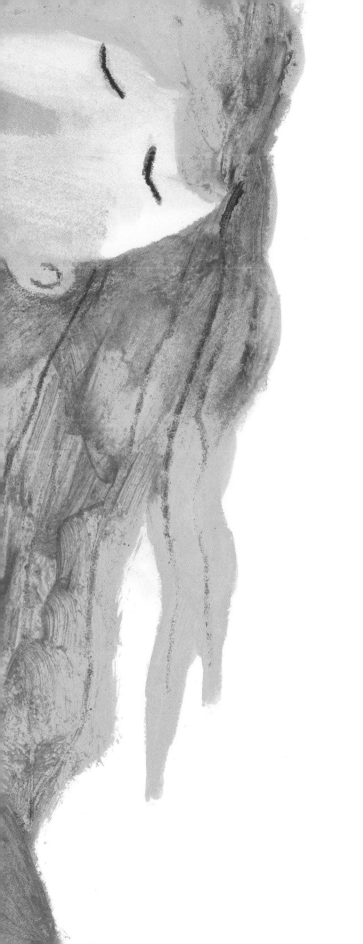

Never.

TO THE ONE WHO THINKS
THAT EVERYTHING FALLS APART

The illustrations for this book were made with oil paint.

Library of Congress Control Number 2019943349

ISBN 978-1-4197-4482-2

First published by hélium/Actes Sud, Paris
© hélium/Actes Sud, 2019
Book design by Max Temescu

Printed and bound in Belgium
10 9 8 7 6 5 4 3 2 1

Abrams Books for Young Readers are available at special discounts when purchased in quantity for premiums and promotions as well as fundraising or educational use. Special editions can also be created to specification. For details, contact specialsales@abramsbooks.com or the address below.

Abrams® is a registered trademark of Harry N. Abrams, Inc.

ABRAMS The Art of Books
195 Broadway, New York, NY 10007
abramsbooks.com